I0669850

Anthony A. C. Shaftesbury

In Memoriam, the Late Earl of Shaftesbury, K.G.,

first president of the Victoria Street Society for the Protection of Animals

from Vivisection

Anthony A. C. Shaftesbury

In Memoriam, the Late Earl of Shaftesbury, K.G.,
first president of the Victoria Street Society for the Protection of Animals from Vivisection

ISBN/EAN: 9783337242930

Printed in Europe, USA, Canada, Australia, Japan

Cover: Foto ©Raphael Reischuk / pixelio.de

More available books at **www.hansebooks.com**

THE MERCIFUL MAN.

In straight and simple lines his pathway ran.
  Little of books he knew. The strifeful
    world
Beyond his circling hills roared on unheard.
  And, so he died—the gnarled, old, work-
    worn man !

His unshaped thought has been—"Alone I've
  lived :
  Alone I've wandered to that life beyond.
Others have friends—wife—children—when I
  come
    To that strange land, O who will welcome
    me ?"

No grieving tears fell when he passed away.
  A hireling's hand arrayed him for the tomb.
A neighbor lingered decently, as fell
  The clods about him in the twilight gray.

Yet, as they fell, along a pathway sped—
  Beneath celestial blooms his boyhood
    knew—
The earth-freed spirit; and about him flew
  The little joyous birds his hands had fed.

And when before a gateway, flower-bespanned,
  He humbly paused, nor dared to pass or
    turn,
A dog he once befriended bounded forth
  And with a joyous whine caressed his hand,

And walked before him, showing him the way,
  The old horse he had loved he too came
    forth.
And pressed his head against his breast
  Uttering a welcome in his gladsome neigh.

And all about him pressed a loving throng,
  Of birds and beasts most gentle-eyed and
    kind.
(Since this new world held neither pain nor
  fear.)
  And all about him rang a joyous song:

"Oh, soul so merciful, we welcome thee !
  Unto all life thou hast been ever kind.
Unto the deathless life we welcome thee !
  Pass on, beloved, and thy rewarding see !

In trembling, thrilling hope he forward passed.
  Before him swung a portal grandly fair.
And the young mother he had never known
  Flew forth and caught him to her yearning
    breast.

Lord Shaftsbury said concerning vivisection: "The thought of this diabolical crime disturbs me night and day."

In Memoriam.

THE LATE

EARL OF SHAFTESBURY, K.G.,

FIRST PRESIDENT

OF THE

Victoria Street Society

FOR THE

Protection of Animals from Vivisection.

LONDON:

Published by the Victoria Street Society for the Protection of
Animals from Vivisection,

UNITED WITH THE

International Association for the Total Suppression of
Vivisection.

1885.

THE STEALTHY ADVANCE OF VIVISECTION.

In the year 1875, in consequence of the cruel experiments which had been published in the works of some English physiologists, a Royal Commission was appointed to inquire into the practice of subjecting live animals to painful experiments for scientific purposes. In their Report the Commissioners express the opinion that "the practice is, from its very nature, liable to great abuse," and say that, "looking to the circumstance that a great increase is to be expected in physiological inquiry, it appears to us most important that some legislative control should be established to prevent abuse extending."

The practical result of this Commission was, that an Act of Parliament was passed in the following year making vivisection illegal, except for specially-licensed persons. It was further provided in the Act that additional certificates might be granted to the operators, permitting them to dispense with the necessity of keeping the animals under the influence of chloroform or other anæsthetics during the operations, and that inspectors should be appointed to visit all registered places. With these results the majority of the public were content, and considered that the question had been satisfactorily and finally settled. A few persons, however, who looked below the surface, foresaw, what has actually proved to be the case, that the Act would be merely a temporary compromise, and, being grounded on no firm moral principle, could not but prove a failure. In fact, it afforded protection, not so much to the animals as to their tormentors, who, provided with licenses and left unvisited by an "inspector" who was one of themselves, were henceforth at liberty to do what they pleased. The number of licenses has been steadily on the increase, and during the last two years it has crept up from thirty-three to fifty-three, and there seems to be no reason why it should not be indefinitely extended, since we have been told that the licenses are granted on the recommendation of an influential scientific society, founded with the express object of protecting the interests of the vivisecting party. Add to this, that some of the experiments during the last ten years have been as cruel as almost any on record, and apparently of no practical use in medicine, and it cannot be said that the endeavour of the Commission to "prevent abuse" has been crowned with success.

On the other hand, their prediction that there would be a great increase in physiological inquiry has been amply fulfilled both here and abroad. Everything now-a-days, be it a fresh drug, a new surgical operation, or merely a fanciful theory, has to be tested on the living animal, and that not by any means to draw conclusions as to the effect on men, but often after it has been used on patients to try what will happen when it is applied to animals. When, in Paris, a man has demonstrated that he can fast for six weeks, a physiologist thinks it an interesting scientific experiment to starve two dogs to the point of death to try how long they can live—the one with water and the other without it—and the *Times* devotes a paragraph to reporting this senseless barbarity, adding a flippant and unfeeling comment.

But the surest sign of the increase in public favour of this practice will be found in the manner in which it has lately been endowed. In 1879 was founded the G. H. Lewes scholarship (value £200 a year) for physiological research, by the aid of which Professor Roy was enabled to perform the agonising experiments which were quoted by Mr. Reid in the House of Commons. Three years ago the University of Oxford voted £10,000 for the erection of a laboratory for Professor Burdon Sanderson, joint editor of the manual which was one of the immediate causes of the appointment of the Royal Commission. It was on account of this act on the part of his University that Professor Ruskin felt called upon to resign his professorship. A few weeks ago only another sum of £10,000 was left by Mr. J. Lucas Walker for the purposes of scientific and literary research. The Attorney-General, into whose hands the bequest was committed, acting on the advice of three friends well known for their advocacy and practice of vivisection, has determined to found with it a studentship for experimental pathology, the holder of which is to be under the immediate control of the above-mentioned Professor Roy.

But the most ominous sign of the times has yet to be told. As is well known, Sir Erasmus Wilson bequeathed upwards of £200,000 to the Royal College of Surgeons for the benefit of their College. In the *British Medical Journal* of January 15th appears a round-robin addressed to the President, Vice-Presidents, and Council of the College, praying that a portion of this sum may be devoted to the erection of an institution like the "splendid laboratories" of Berlin, Paris, Leipzig, &c. Of the fifty-two scientific men by whom this memorial has been signed, thirty-one, at least, have either actually practised vivisection or have publicly advocated the practice, and demanded the repeal of the present law; nineteen of them have held licenses, of whom seventeen have had the additional certificate dispensing with the necessity for keeping the animals unconscious of their sufferings.

The natures and opinions of these gentlemen may be seen from the following facts. One of them has recently performed a series of experiments which consisted in cutting open the abdomens of living animals, laying bare the kidneys, dissecting out, cutting, and tying the ends of all the most sensitive nerves, and stimulating them with electricity, to try what effect that would have on the circulation of the kidney. Another has exposed portions of the brains of cats and other animals, and applied electricity to them till the animals uttered "long-continued cries as if of rage and pain." A third has kept the ear of one living animal in the stomach of another for four hours and a half, until the action of the gastric juice had completely eaten away a portion of it. A fourth has killed animals by the application of external heat until their temperature was seventeen degrees above blood heat, which cannot be said to differ much from baking them alive. A fifth has written: "The rocks are broken and put in the crucible, the water is submitted to analysis, the plant is dissected. . . . . In animal life the same method must be adopted to unlock the secrets of nature. *The question of the animal being sensitive cannot alter the mode of investigation.*" A sixth has openly announced that he has no regard for the sufferings of the animals, and that he does not think there is any difference on this point among the physiologists of England.

From such specimens, which but for want of space might be multiplied, it would be evident what kind of laboratory is likely to be established, had not those of Berlin, Leipzig, and Paris, been specially named, and had not mention been made of the investigations for the prevention of hydrophobia—investigations which for heartless cruelty can hardly be surpassed, since in the words of their author the dreadful disease, "the very thought of which strikes one with fear," has been communicated to so many animals that "they have passed beyond the possibility of numbering them."

We fear it is only too probable that the College will be disposed to grant the petition of this influentially signed memorial, but still hope that so strong a public protest may be made that they will pause before they bring the disgrace on themselves and on our country, which has ever been the first to defend the innocent and help the helpless, of introducing into our midst the elaborate appliances and wholesale horrors of the foreign laboratory, which even the advocates of vivisection have hitherto agreed in condemning.

E. B.

—From *Church Bells*, January 28, 1887.

[Since the above was published the *British Medical Journal* (Feb. 19) has announced two further endowments of Vivisection. viz., the " Foundation of a Research Laboratory by the College of Physicians of Edinburgh " (p. 414), and the sanction by the Senate of the University of Cambridge, of the " preparation of plans for a Physiological Laboratory, the whole cost of which is estimated at £10,000 " (p. 402)].

Published by the VICTORIA STREET SOCIETY FOR THE PROTECTION OF ANIMALS FROM VIVISECTION, UNITED WITH THE INTERNATIONAL ASSOCIATION FOR THE TOTAL SUPPRESSION OF VIVISECTION, 1, VICTORIA STREET, WESTMINSTER, S.W.   11.87.

RECORD.

LORD SHAFTESBURY never joined the Victoria Street Society ; it was the Society which joined Lord SHAFTESBURY. There was a day in November, 1875, when, having telegraphed his readiness to support the project of Dr. HOGGAN and Miss COBBE, he, in fact, founded the Society. It was around him, and attracted in great part by his name, that the whole body eventually gathered. A brief record may here be given of his subsequent services to the Anti-Vivisection Cause.

It was at the third meeting of the Executive Committee, on the 18th February, 1876, in Dr. Hoggan's house in Granville Place, that Lord SHAFTESBURY for the first time occupied the Chair. He again took it (vacating it on the entry of the Archbishop of YORK) on the 1st March, when the "*Statement*" of the Society was formally adopted. Shortly afterwards he consented to be elected President ; and thenceforth practically directed all the public action of the Society, and such of its interior concerns as the Hon.Sec. thought it desirable to submit to him for counsel.

On the 20th March, 1876, he headed a great Deputation to the Home Office to press on Mr. (now Sir Richard) Cross the introduction into Parliament of a Bill in accordance with the recommendations of the Royal Commission. Among the members of this deputation were Colonel (now Sir EVELYN) WOOD, Cardinal MANNING, the Earl of MINTO, Sir FREDERICK ELLIOT, Right Hon. A. J. MUNDELLA, Mr. FROUDE, Mr. LESLIE STEPHEN, and Lord MOUNT-TEMPLE. The prayer of the Memorial of this deputation having been acceded to by the HOME SECRETARY, Lord SHAFTESBURY again presided at a meeting of the Committee, and framed suggestions which, on being presented to Sir RICHARD CROSS, were embodied under his direction in Lord CARNARVON's Bill. In support of this Bill in the House of Lords, on the 22nd May, 1876,

Lord SHAFTESBURY made his first great speech for our Cause. It was a long address, occupying a pamphlet of 22 pages, and in it he displayed an exhaustive study of the then recently issued Minutes of Evidence of the Royal Commission, and also of the arguments employed by the advocates of vivisection. He told the Government that "the feeling of the country was in favour of total abolition; but that he was prepared to accept the Bill which only imposed restriction." Lord SHAFTESBURY proceeded to give in brief but very telling language descriptions of the hideous experiments of BRACHET and others, and quoted largely from the Blue-book. It was in this great speech that Lord SHAFTESBURY introduced the phrase of *Chamber Sport*, which illustrates so well the antithesis between the vivisections of the physiological laboratory and the injuries inflicted on animals in the open fields by the hunter and fowler.

On the 1st of June, 1876, Lord SHAFTESBURY presided at the first Annual Meeting of the Society, at which Lord BUTE, Lord GLASGOW, and Cardinal MANNING took part. Confident hopes were, at that time, entertained that Lord CARNARVON's Bill would be passed by the House of Commons in the shape in which it had come from the House of Lords —a shape which would have almost secured the objects of the Society. By that Bill, as it then stood, experiments on dogs, cats, horses, asses, and mules were absolutely forbidden; no certificates would have permitted them to anybody; and all experiments on other animals were required to be performed under complete anæsthesia;—conditions which would have practically put an end to Vivisection as a Method of Research. Unhappily, as our readers know, a great Medical Deputation, got up by certain wire-pullers of the profession, invaded the Home Office on the 10th of July, and placed such pressure on Mr. CROSS as to cause him to eviscerate the Bill (then in his hands for presentation to the House of Commons) and leave it the mangled and illogical measure which, on the 15th of August, became by royal signature, the Vivisection Act, 39 & 40 Vict., c. 77. In replying, a few days later, to a letter written to him by the

Hon. Sec. in deep dejection and disappointment, Lord SHAFTESBURY explained why he had consented to allow this mangled Bill to pass rather than let it fall to the ground. After mentioning that he had had an interview with Mr. CROSS about the changes in the Bill which he deplored, he went on to say, "But the question then was simply 'the Bill as propounded, or no Bill,' for Mr. CROSS stoutly maintained that without the alterations suggested, he had no hope of carrying anything at all. I reverted, therefore, to my first opinion, stated at the very commencement of my co-operation with your Committee, that it was of great importance, nay indispensable, to obtain a Bill, however imperfect, which should condemn the practice, put a limit on the exercise of it, and give us a foundation on which to build amendments hereafter as time and opportunity should be offered to us." (August 16th, 1876.)

From that period the policy of the Society, as settled by a resolution of the Committee, November 22nd, was to watch the enforcement of the Act and keep in view its extension to the total prohibition of vivisection. On this ground Lord SHAFTESBURY warmly approved next spring the support of Mr. HOLT's (Total Abolition) Bill and the exhibition by the Society of the well-known illustrated posters over the hoardings of London. He presided at the Second Annual Meeting on April 27th, 1877, at which the Bishop of WINCHESTER and Lord MOUNT-TEMPLE took part—the latter having shown from the first, and next to Lord SHAFTESBURY, the deepest interest in the work of the Society. The third assembly of the Society Lord SHAFTESBURY received in his own house in Grosvenor Square on the 23rd February, 1878. In the August following the Society formally adopted the principle of total abolition, and Lord SHAFTESBURY wrote to the Hon. Sec. on her announcement of the fact as follows :— (Sept. 3rd, 1878), "Your letter is very cheering. We were right to make the experiment. We were right to test the men and the law, Mr. CROSS and his administration of it. Both have failed us, and we are bound in duty, I think, to leap over all limitations, and go in for the total abolition of this vile and cruel form of idolatry, for idolatry it is, and like all idolatry, brutal, degrading, and deceptive." . . .

On the 15th July Lord TRURO having presented his Bill in the House of Lords, Lord SHAFTESBURY made, in supporting it, the second speech printed in the following pages. No more affecting sight could well be witnessed than that of the aged philanthropist who for sixty years had pleaded for justice for all classes of human sufferers, standing up once more among his peers to ask for mercy to brutes; his voice faltering as he described their tortures. Writing of the debate on the 16th July he said :—"Defeated, you see, by 6 to 1. . . . All the papers seem full of contempt and hatred. . . . Carnarvon voted against us. I had almost hoped that he and some others would have stayed away. But we have done our best, at least I did mine, and that 'best' being but small, was only instrumental in obtaining 16 votes." And again on July 18th he added, "Some good will come out of the discussion. I have unmistakeable evidence that many were deeply impressed. But obedience to political leaders is a higher law with most politicians than obedience to truth."

The Annual Meeting for 1880 was held at the house (8, Cromwell Houses) of those generous friends of the Society, Mr. and Mrs. FRANK MORRISON; and the President again took the chair. A few days later he presented to Mr. GLADSTONE the important Memorial, signed by 100 representative men—Peers, Judges, General Officers, and Heads of Colleges, &c.—to which Mr. GLADSTONE of course replied, expressing his (unfortunately still inactive) sympathy. The Meeting of 1881, at the house of Lord COLERIDGE; that of 1882 at his own house; that of 1883 at 1, Grosvenor Place; of 1884 at Prince's Hall; and of 1885, at the Westminster Palace Hotel, were, every one of them, presided over by Lord SHAFTESBURY; who also took the Chair at two Meetings of the East London and North London Branches of the Society. Beside all these more public assemblies, Lord SHAFTESBURY took the utmost pains to attend the meetings of the Executive Committee, appointing with great care the

days and hours left to him by his other innumerable engage-
ments, and never once failing to keep his promise. His
signature appears on the Minute-Book of the Committee no
less than 49 times. It may be added that in none of the
council rooms of the charitable bodies, great and small, where
he worked, did Lord SHAFTESBURY show himself more full of
consideration for everyone co-operating with him, more genial
and friendly, and more completely devoid of the *morgue*,
of which the *Times* has accused him, than in the Committee Room of Victoria Street. Punctual to the moment,
he always entered with the kindest of greetings for each
member present, and rarely failed to linger for general con-
versation when the business of the day was done—an
extraordinary amount of business having been usually got
through in an hour or two under his guidance. Nor did he
only give his invaluable counsels on such occasions. He often
called at the office on other days beside those of the Committee, and was at all times ready to receive and advise the
Secretaries, either in personal interviews at his house, or by
letter. The late Hon. Sec. now possesses 260 such letters
to her in his own handwriting, filled, for the most part, with
wise advice and the kindest sympathy and encouragement.

But in truth, the actual work done by Lord SHAFTESBURY
for the Anti-Vivisection Cause, great as it was, constituted
only a small part of the support he gave it by lending it the
authority of his great character, and infusing into it his lofty
and religious spirit. A General may never fire a shot or strike a
blow in a battle, but the victory may nevertheless be entirely
due to his presence among the troops. It is not too much to say
that it has been the spirit of this righteous man—who "feared
God, and feared nothing else,"—this man with a single eye
to justice, and no side views to self-indulgence or self-interest,
which has infused itself into, and more or less thoroughly
inspired, the whole party of Anti-vivisectionists. While the
apologists of scientific cruelty have been outbidding one
another in their appeals to human cowardice, and in their
efforts to coax their countrymen to condone their hateful

cruelties by dangling before them glittering promises, the members of Lord SHAFTESBURY's Society have one and all struck a higher note—feebly no doubt, but never falsely,— "What if it *be* possible to relieve our maladies by methods involving cruelty and sin? Not therefore will cruelty and sin be less abominable." While the physiologists told us that the lower animals are our brothers in blood, and akin to us in sensibility to pain, and in the same breath called on us to consent to their barbarous torture—Lord SHAFTESBURY never failed to remind us that the brutes are the creatures of our Father in Heaven; and this thought has quickened every effort of ours to save them, and has daily bent the knees of more than ten thousand men and women in prayer for GOD's assistance in our work.

He is gone. We shall never see him, nor yet his like, again. When the whole Society rose at the annual meeting last July, to do him honour as he left the room, sad forebodings must have been in many hearts that he had occupied his seat for the last time, and spoken his last words; that his venerable yet stately figure, his voice, enfeebled by age, but resonant still with courage and feeling, would be seen and heard amongst those who so loved and honoured him, no more. But though the end has come even sooner than was feared, there is comfort in the thought that the long, sad twilight of senility never fell on that vigorous brain, and that he was spared both bodily pain and the infirmities of failing senses. For *him* to have survived his powers of usefulness would have been a terrible misfortune. A year before his death, having spoken to the writer of these pages concerning the suffering of women and girls, he said, "When I feel age creeping on me and know I must soon die,—I hope it is not wrong to say it,—but *I cannot bear to leave the world with all the misery in it.*" Thus he, who if any man might do so, looked forward with confidence to entering at death "into the joy of his Lord," yet wished to live, because he could do somewhat to relieve the misery of man and woman and child and brute. Other men have desired to remain in the world because of the pleasures it offers them; and others again have wished to quit a scene so full of anguish and injustice. But Lord SHAFTESBURY wished to live, *because of the misery of the world!*

This was the man who was our Leader. In his spirit we must continue to work, each as our powers permit. He will, we believe, remember the objects of his earthly sympathy where he is ; and perhaps to such spirits as his it may be granted still to help the wretchedness which they pitied here in other, higher ways than the methods of our poor world. But at least it is our part to struggle on in his footsteps ; to take care that his labours in our cause shall not fail ; to hold aloft the same noble standard of principle which he carried before us, and to strive to the goal of his longings and our own—the final triumph of Mercy over false science and selfish cruelty.

F. P. C.

OCTOBER, 1885.

THE LATE LORD SHAFTESBURY'S VIEWS ON VIVISECTION.

As a Memorial of the late lamented President of the Victoria Street Society, and as a record of the strength of his opinions on the Vivisection question and the vigour with which he expressed them on two great occasions, we here reprint his Speeches in the House of Lords.

The first is the substance of a speech delivered in the House of Lords, Monday, 22nd May, 1876, in support of Lord Carnarvon's Bill.

The Earl of SHAFTESBURY said the Bill did not go as far as could be wished, but, nevertheless, he desired to thank the Government for bringing it in. The excitement throughout the country was very great, as was shown by the Petitions that had been addressed to Parliament; and they would have been more numerous and forcible if the people had not believed that the Government would legislate on the Report of the Commission. To show the strength of the feeling which he believed predominated in the country, he would quote the language of one Petition, which was as follows:—

"That your Petitioners, feeling that cruel experiments are on no grounds justifiable, hereby humbly entreat your Honourable House to legislate for the total abolition and utter suppression of what is termed 'vivisection,' or the cutting-up of living creatures, or otherwise torturing them, or putting them to death by torture, under any scientific pretext whatsoever. Perpetrators of these atrocities allege that they physically benefit mankind, though competent authorities deny the assertion. But, even if it were so, no physical gain can possibly equal the injury caused by the moral degradation of the feelings which such barbarous experiments must naturally induce."

The supporters of the Government measure would, he feared, be misrepresented, or, at least, misunderstood, for it could not be denied that the feeling of the country was in favour of total abolition ; but, knowing the difficulties which surrounded the question, he was prepared to accept the Bill, which only imposed restrictions ; and he did it upon this ground—that while he believed restriction might be effective he feared that abolition would be a dead letter. Now, if it had been difficult to obtain evidence before the Royal Commission for information, how much more difficult would it be to obtain evidence for a prosecution when all the men of science were opposed to the measure. All sorts of arguments were urged against interference, but he had heard none so groundless as those of the noble Duke. Field-sports might be justifiable or unjustifiable, though he had nothing to do with such sports. The argument was not applicable to him. He never hunted a fox in his life ; many years ago he hunted a hare, and he then determined from that time never to do so again. But he would not go into the question of field-sports at all. They were beside the question. One evil, supposing this to be an evil, did not palliate another. Was it not permitted to abate suffering, though it could not be extinguished altogether ? Common sense drew a distinction between them and prolonged deliberate mutilation, the submitting of animals to torture from hour to hour and month to month. The argument derived from field-sports was, if good at all, good only against those who hunted, and it was no argument whatever to the mass of the people of these lands, who never hunted, and who yet were the Petitioners that demanded these prohibitions. But, if the amusements of the fine folk of England were to be quoted as reasons why there should be no restriction on vivisection, let those amusements be contrasted with the amusements of the vivisectors, with that continuous excitement of morbid curiosity which found its employment and recreation in ingenious and prolonged suffering. M. Brachet, an eminent French physician under Charles X. and Louis Philippe, who obtained the physiological prize from the Institute, narrated the following experiment :—

"I inspired a dog,"—he begged noble Lords to observe the rich language of science,—"I inspired a dog with the greatest aversion for me by plaguing and inflicting some pain or other upon it as often as I saw it." Here was a precious pursuit of knowledge! "When this feeling was carried to its height, so that the animal became furious as soon as it saw or heard me, I put out its eyes ; I could then appear before it without its manifesting any aversion." What a discovery! "I spoke, and immediately its barkings and furious movements proved the passion which animated it. I destroyed the drum of its ears, and disorganised the internal ear as much as I could." This was the language of absolute relish. "When an intense inflammation which was excited had rendered it deaf, I filled up its ears with wax. It could no longer hear at all. Then I went to its side, spoke aloud, and even caressed it, without its falling into a rage; it seemed even sensible to my caresses." What a heart the man must have had! It was thought necessary to repeat this experiment, in order that there might be no uncertainty in the result." "And what," observes Dr. Elliotson, who criticised the case, "was all this to prove? Simply that if one brute has an aversion to another it does not feel or show that aversion when it has no means of knowing that the other brute is present. If he had stood near the dog on the other side of a wall, he might have equally proved what common sense required not to be proved. I blush for human nature in detailing this experiment." Dr. Elliotson wrote well. Why did not every man blush who heard of it? And here let the amusements of the French physiologist be compared with that of a day's fox-hunting!

It might be said this was a foreign practice; but what was the testimony of Sir William Fergusson, that great and eminent surgeon? He said, "The impression on my mind is that these experiments are done in the most reckless and shocking manner." He added, "I will give you an illustration of an animal being crucified for several days, the poor animal being brought in day after day for several days merely that the spectators might see the progress of its suffering." What was this but sheer amusement? Could science have gained by a cold-blooded, systematic cruelty such as this, one hair's breadth of knowledge for the use of mankind?—This perhaps was gained; a proof was gained of what men can bring themselves to do when science is degraded to a wretched monomania. Sir William was asked if he believed that much of this was going on, and his answer was, "I believe a great deal of reckless mutilation is going on among students even in private; houses." Well, all sorts of objections had been urged, heavy and light. Seal-skins, it was stated, were obtained by reckless means. Now, first, an effort had been made by law to appoint proper seasons for the seal-fishing—and, secondly, this argument was effective only against those who wore that kind of fur, and not against the millions who, dressing in cotton and woollens, demanded that animals should be protected. He himself (Lord Shaftesbury) in a controversy he had with a distinguished man—an eminent surgeon—when he was urging on him the necessity of moderation and care in physiological experimentation, received for reply, that he must look at home and ask himself if he did not indulge in *pâté de foie gras* [pie of goose-livers artificially enlarged]. Why, he, and the masses who sympathised with him, had never tasted *pâté de foie gras* in their lives, and probably never should taste it. All he could say was, *pâté de foie gras* brought its own punishment with it—being as indigestible as it was wicked.

Now, this evil of vivisection was extended over the whole of Europe, and was beginning to be very rife in this country.

Dr. Haughton, on this point, fully confirmed the testimony of Sir William Fergusson, and stated—

"I believe that a large proportion of the experiments now performed upon animals in England, Scotland, and Ireland are unnecessary, and clumsy repetitions of well-known results. Young physiologists in England learn German and read experiments in German journals, and repeat them in this country. There is a good deal of that second-rate sort of physiological practice going on;" all of which their Lordships might believe was as useless as it was atrocious.

Now, if vivisection had been exhibited to their Lordships for the first time, all would have shrunk from it with abhorrence; but now, suddenly, they were confronted with a long-established system; and they had to deal with the arguments and facts of learned men of very various dispositions. Vivisection was urged as a grand necessity for the prolongation of human life and the alleviation of human suffering. Doubtless, there were many and great names in favour of the practice, but there were also great names who questioned the necessity, and hesitated to believe that any real good had resulted atall in proportion to the thousands of hecatombs of animals that had been slaughtered and tortured in this terrible pursuit of science.

Sir WILLIAM FERGUSSON observed that—

"Mr. Syme lived to express an abhorrence of such operations,—at all events, if they were not useful. His ultimate authority was strongly on the other side (against them), as was expressed in a special report of his own. No man, perhaps," said Sir William, "has ever had more experience of the human subject than Mr. Syme, and I myself have a strong opinion that such an expression, coming from Mr. Syme, was a mature and valuable opinion." When asked whether his own opinion in mature life was much less favourable to these experiments than when he was young, "Yes," he replied, "because I had not the same grasp of the subject at that time. I was more, perhaps, influenced by what other people had done, and by the wish to come up to what they had done, in such matters; but the more mature judgment of recent years has led me to say to myself now that I would not perform some of the operations at this present time that I performed myself in earlier days." This was of weight.

Professor ROLLESTON stated—

"Haller fell in his later age into a permanent anguish of conscience, which is shown in his epistles, reproaching himself most bitterly for his vivisections (stated by Krug). I think I may say this (but I shall not give the name), that it is within my own personal experience that a person who has a considerable name before the world, and has performed a large number of vivisections in his time, has expressed himself to me as exceedingly sorry that he ever did them—did them, I should say, to the extent to which he did."

To these might be added the names of Dr. Child. Dr. Crisp, and others. But further. In the life of that accomplished man, Sir Charles Bell, was to be found this passage :—

"In his study of the system of circulation, as in that of the nerves, Charles Bell was necessarily compelled to make more than one experiment in comparative anatomy; but he abstained as much as possible from torturing animals, which he considered, in most cases, a useless act of cruelty, less certain in result than was commonly supposed, and less profitable than an attentive study of pathological phenomena, because vivisection (not only alters the substance of the mutilated organs, but disturbs, more or less profoundly, the natural condition of life, and excites, through pain, irregular motions differing from those expected or previously observed, &c." Why, this passage was almost an answer to the whole inquiry; not only did he avoid torture, so far as he could, but he considered the study of pathology superior to the practice of vivisection.—But here was, no doubt, the difference in the minds of the experimentalists; pathology was long, and vivisection was short; study a bore, but action an amusement. " Sir Charles admitted that his own opinion was not the opinion of some of the best and most virtuous men he had ever known, but that for his own part he could never convince himself either by the experiments he witnessed or by any of those related to him."

What a testimony from such a man !

But he wished particularly to call their Lordships attention to a letter written by Sir Charles Bell himself :—

" I should be writing," he said, " a third paper on the nerves, but I cannot proceed without making some experiments, which are so unpleasant to make that I defer them. You may think me silly "—would their Lordships mark these words?— "but I cannot perfectly convince myself that I am authorized in nature or religion to do these cruelties:" would they pause here for a minute. Sir Charles proceeded, and "for what?" he said. " For anything else than a little egotism or self-aggrandisement? and yet, what are my experiments in comparison with those which are daily done, and are done daily for nothing ? " Their Lordships might be assured that the people of England rested their hatred—no lighter term can be used of this terrible system—on the grounds suggested by Sir Charles Bell. It was with many of them not simply a matter of feeling, it was one of religion. He (Lord S.) did not believe that it could be eradicated ; he hardly believed that it could be partially subdued. A violent unqualified opposition to their wishes might bring on such expressions of sentiment as would end in the most coercive measures, and the formation of a public opinion, hostile alike to science and to scientific men personally, in the matter of vivisection.

But this Bill did not demand the solution of the

difficulty whether vivisection were really necessary or not; it went only to the extent to which the men of science would go in limitation of an acknowledged evil. Now his noble friend had stated facts. He would add one or two. It was impossible to describe the feelings they excited. The narrator in this instance was M. Bouillaud, a man of high scientific name, and one of the most conspicuous physicians in the Medical School of Paris. The account of the eleventh experiment began thus:—

"I made an opening on each side of the forehead of a young dog, and forced a red hot iron into each of the anterior lobes of the brain"—would their Lordships observe the light jaunty way in which he relates his chamber sport? "Immediately afterwards, the animal, after howling violently, lay down as if to sleep. On urging it, it walked or even ran for a considerable space; it did not know how to avoid obstacles placed in its way, and on encountering them groaned, or even howled violently. Deprived of the knowledge of external objects, it no longer made any movements either to avoid or approach them." As if common sense would not have taught this to any one. "But it still could perform such motions as are called instinctive. It withdrew its feet when they were pinched, and shook itself when water was poured upon it. It turned incessantly in the cage as if to get out, and became impatient of the restraint thus imposed."

After noting many revolting details, he said:—

"It slept occasionally for a short time, and on awakening began its mournful cries. We tried to keep it quiet by beating it, but it only cried more loudly. It did not understand the lesson; it was incorrigible." What stuff! to say nothing of his feelings; was the man in his senses?

Some days elapsed and the journal continued :—

" Its fore-legs are now half paralysed in walking, 'or rather in dragging itself along ; it rests upon the back of its foot, bent upon the leg. No change has taken place in respect to his intellectual power ; as its irrepressible cries disturbed the neighbourhood I was obliged to kill it." Here the atrocious prolongation of torture should be noted.

This gentleman was insatiable ; he presented another rich experiment, rich in showing what men can do and what animals must submit to. Another young dog, so went the narrative, that had been exposed to similar suffering from having had " the cranium and cerebral hemispheres sawed transversely," escaped from its torturer by a comparatively easy death. " To prevent its plaintive cries disturbing my neighbours,"—what humane consideration ! " I enveloped it in a thick sack. On examining some time afterwards, I found that it had died from suffocation." Another dog was selected, " possessing the reputation of being lively, docile, and intelligent." The anterior part of its brain was transfixed on the 28th of June, and day after day, for several weeks, it was tortured in every possible way, and the effects recorded. After detailing the results, he says, on the 7th of July :—

" When menanced it crouches, as if to implore mercy "—could anything, except a demi-fiend, have felt or written in that way ?—" but it does not in consequence obey. It, on the contrary, utters cries which nothing can repress, similar to those of an uneducated dog, whose intellect is undeveloped." What did their Lordships think the dog would have replied to the developed intellect of his torturer, could he have spoken ? The very dumbness of the animals should be a powerful appeal on their behalf.

"I watched attentively," he went on, "for the remainder of this and for the first fifteen days of the succeeding month." The ferocious prolongation of suffering should again be observed.

But to sum up, in the words of Dr. Walker, let them listen to a choice category of experimental recreations.

"Forcing substances into the stomach of a dog after exposing the gullet, and tying it to prevent vomiting; opening the abdomen, tying a portion of the small intestine in two places, opening the intermediate portion, and injecting a noxious fluid into it; starving rabbits till they would eat dead frogs; forcing boiling water into a dog's stomach; boiling frogs; starving pigeons till they dropped from their perches, and then cutting of their anterior or posterior extremities to show that this caused death when the organism was exhausted from want of food." Did man, from all this, walk in greater honour and greater security? and was it not now clear to their Lordships that they ought to do something to put a check upon such wild, wanton, and superfluous cruelties? Now let them hear Dr. Acland, a very eminent physician—what did he say?

"The number of persons in this and other countries who are becoming biologists without being medical men is very much increasing. Modern civilization seems to be set upon acquiring biological knowledge, and one of the consequences of this is, that, whereas medical men are constantly engaged in the study of anatomy and physiology for a humane purpose (that is, for the purpose of doing immediate good to mankind), there are a number of persons now who are engaged in the pursuit of these subjects for the purpose of acquiring abstract knowledge. That is quite a different thing. I am not at all sure that the mere acquisition of knowledge is not a thing having some dangerous and mischievous tendencies in it. . . ." That very striking and most true observation deserved serious attention. "Now it has become a profession," he continued, "to discover, and to discover at any cost."

Mr. G. H. LEWES said :—

"One man discovers a fact or publishes an experiment, and instantly, all over Europe, certain people set to work to repeat it. They will repeat it, and repeat it, and repeat it." Mr. Lewes was right. Unless checked, they will repeat any amount of cruelty without the slightest addition of knowledge.

Dr. HAUGHTON said :—

"I would shrink with horror from accustoming large classes of young men to the sight of animals under vivisection. I believe that many of them would become cruel and hardened, and would go away and repeat those experiments recklessly. Science would gain nothing, and the world would have let loose upon it a set of young devils." Was not, he asked their Lordships, the great rush of them already begun?

Dr. ANTHONY, another high testimony, "knew himself of instances of young men, from mere curiosity, carrying on these experiments. Could mention them, but would scarcely like to do so. No anæsthetics are used to diminish the pain of the creatures." Of course not, it would be too much trouble. Respecting demonstrations by professors to students, Dr. Anthony says :—"I believe the more you keep the scenic element away the better. The reason is the existence of a morbid curiosity. There is a morbid curiosity which is known to medical men well with reference to operations of all kinds." That was just what had been asserted all along,

"There are a certain number of persons who are very fond of coming to see the different operations at the hospitals. I look upon that, and particularly upon the desire of seeing these experiments on animals as something very, very morbid indeed."

Could anything, he asked their Lordships, be more illustrative than the written statement put in by Mr. James B. Mills?—

"Observing from the daily papers that Mr. Ernest Hart alleges that students do not perform experiments on living, animals as an exercise in the prosecution of their studies, I beg to forward to you a summary of my experience in that respect during my college career at Edinburgh. I am a veterinary surgeon, and I feel it my duty to aid your Society in repressing unnecessary experimentation; surveying the past as I do, with much regret, so far as I have participated in the practices which I am now compelled to condemn. At Edinburgh the veterinary students and the medical students frequently associate for pleasure and for study. The experiments were certainly never designed to discover any new fact, or elucidate any obscure phenomena, but simply to demonstrate the most ordinary facts of physiology. Our victims were sometimes dogs, but more frequently cats. Many of the latter were caught by means of a poisoned bait, the animals being secured whilst suffering from the agonies caused by the poison, when antidotes were applied for their restoration. They were then imprisoned in a cupboard at the students' lodgings, and kept there until a meeting could be arranged. Sometimes the students secured their victims by what is known as a cat-hunt, that is, a raid on cats by students armed with sticks late at night. I am not prepared to say that the object of the students was to commit cruelty, or that there was any morbid desire to witness pain, but I say emphatically that there was no other motive than idle curiosity and heedless, reckless love of experimentation. What, for instance, could justify the following experiment, performed for the purpose of witnessing the action of a cat's heart? The operator first of all made an incision through the skin of the animal's chest, extending from the neck to the belly. The skin was then laid back by hooks, in order to enable the operator to cut through the cartilage of the breast-bone, and to draw his knife across the ribs for the purpose of nicking them. This process is necessary to enable him to snap the ribs and lay the fractured parts back, which also are secured with hooks. It is needless to say that such operation is a most cruel one; but it is only one of several others performed at Edinburgh. Now, the action of the heart is well-known, and is one of the first things taught to students of physiology, and can be taught as well without experimentation as with. In a few cases the animals were narcotised, when no suffering was caused either in the process of poisoning or in the after experimentations." The repetition, then, their Lordships would see, was for diversion, not for knowledge. "The securing an animal for an operation like the above requires experience and care, and it is fearful to witness the struggles of the animal while this is being done. I desire to exonerate the professors from any participation in the experiments performed by students, which were conducted at the private lodgings of students, when none but students were present."

On cross-examination, Mr. Mills confirmed these statements. He said :—

"The experiments" (made chiefly on cats and dogs) " had no other motive than idle curiosity and reckless love of experimentation." All the students (a class of seventy or eighty) assisted more or less at these useless experiments. They were sometimes done in public in the yard of the college. "The habit of doing such things is sure to go on unless a stop is put to it." He referred to a special case which occurred last winter session. A horse was bought for the purpose of dissection. This animal was subjected during a whole week to various operations, such as tenotomy and neurotomy, &c. The operations were "very painful." No anæsthetics of any kind were given. The experiments were made "all over the animal." Edinburgh, it was clear, would soon be a match for Paris in competitive examinations on animal torture. "A dog, too, which was first half-poisoned and then restored by an antidote, received ' brutal usage.' The brains were knocked out by a hammer."

The story of the horse was subsequently confirmed by Principal Williams.

Dr. Scott, also, may be heard on the easy indifference of these lovers of scientific truth.

After describing how he ceased to attend the physiological lectures in Edinburgh on account of the cruelty he witnessed, he says that "it did not provoke the slightest symptoms of abhorrence among those who witnessed it." He "never knew an operation cause the least abhorrence to a medical student." Vivisection, he believes, goes on among students in their own rooms.

But few things had alarmed him more than something he saw lately in the Text-book of the Science and Art Department of the Committee of Council on Education, a book entitled "Lessons in Elementary Physiology," by Thomas Huxley, LL.D., F.R.S. Had he not seen it he could hardly have believed it possible, strange and numerous as were the novel things that sprang up every day.

In the preface to the first edition Professor Huxley says :—

"The following 'Lessons in Elementary Physiology' are primarily intended to serve the purpose of a text-book for teachers and learners in boys' and girls' schools."

In the next place it is strongly insisted " that such experiments as those subjoined shall not merely be studied in the manual, but actually repeated, either by the ' boys and girls ' themselves, or else by the teacher in their presence, as plainly appears from the preface to the second edition. There it was said, ' the knowledge ' which is ' attainable by mere reading, though infinitely better than ignorance,' yet loses ' almost its whole worth as an intellectual discipline' to those who seek it only in books. Where then could it be sought but in the living animal?" And the last phrase showed it by asserting the necessity of the knowledge " arising from direct contact with fact."

But that there might be no doubt, he asked their Lordships' attention to the passage in the ninth edition, page 52:—" If in a rabbit," the Professor stated, "the sympathetic nerve which sends branches to the vessels of the head is cut, the ear of the rabbit . . . . at once blushes . . . . To produce pallor and cold in the rabbit's ear, it is only necessary to irritate the cut end of the sympathetic." It was manifest that the incision to make the ear of the rabbit blush must be on the living, and not on the dead animal.*

* Note.—Professor Huxley has since written to *The Times* to disclaim all intention of advising vivisection by teachers and learners.

And was that the way, he asked, to bring up children? Was that the progress we had made in the nineteenth century? From ignorance, perhaps, the tendency of children was to be cruel, and who did not know the necessity of daily rebuke to check that propensity? But under this unprecedented scheme of intellectual training they were to be accustomed, from their earliest years, not only to witness, but to inflict, agonies of pain on the poor helpless creatures they should be taught to love and protect. Sir Astley Cooper must have been brought up after this fashion. In his Life by his nephew, Bransby Cooper, we read the following story:—

"During this time, Astley, who was always eager to add to our anatomical and physiological knowledge, made a variety of experiments on living animals. I recollect one day walking out with him, when a dog followed us and accompanied us home," mark this—the dog is taught by nature to confide in man, "little foreseeing the fate that awaited him. He was confined for a few days, till we had ascertained that no owner would come to claim him, and then brought up to be the subject of various operations. The first of these was the tying one of the femoral arteries. When poor," mark the pity! "poor Chance, for so we appropriately named the dog, was sufficiently recovered from this"—mark the brutality of that tender care, to cure him for further suffering! "one of the humeral arteries was subjected to a similar process. After the lapse of a few weeks the ill-fated animal was killed, the vessels injected, and preparations were made from each of the limbs. It appears," the biographer continued, "that the dogs sacrificed in my uncle's scientific researches were not unfrequently procured in this manner." That was, as the biographer had stated elsewhere, by agents, who obtained the animals by every form of illicit art. "Nothing but the objects which led to these delinquencies," added the historian, "could offer an excuse for such proceedings." And so they had there, as elsewhere, the full indulgence of the precept, that the end justifies the means.

But he (Lord S.) must go further. He did not know whether their Lordships would hesitate to join him in believing that in such an ardent adoration of science, worshipped and pursued under the high pretext of the universal alleviation of human suffering, pursued for discoveries that were to raise man's intellect by perpetual progress in this kind of knowledge, with an increasing relish for it, the step was very narrow between the vivisection of the animal and the vivisection of the human being. It had been so in old times; it might be so again. Dr. Macaulay, in his valuable work, " Plea for Mercy to Animals," said that the system prevailed in the days of Celsus, in a time of refinement, and what is termed high civilization—Celsus wrote with horror of the cruelties perpetrated on living men and living women. But the world was returning, he (Lord S.) said, to many of the opinions of those earlier days; and why not, then, to their practices? This was no mere conjecture. It was to be recollected that Cheselden, one of the most distinguished surgeons of the last century, wishing to investigate a surgical question, had proposed to try the experiment on a criminal condemned to death, but the opposition which was manifested on this occasion prevented his desire being carried into effect. That was good; but people became familiar very soon with strange things often proposed; and science at that time had not then, as now, been deified. But something was dawning even in modern minds. The testimony of Dr. Rutherford gave cause for disquietude. "In your judgment," he was asked, "are operations of that description upon the dog to be taken as evidence of what the effect would be on a human being?" "Certainly not; but merely as suggesting what the action would be, that is all. The experiment must also be tried upon men before a conclusion can be drawn." Exactly so; and if in the fanatical authority of science, and the equally fanatical obedience to it, some conclusions were declared to be absolutely necessary, criminals, as heretofore, might be utilized for the purpose—for, though scientific men were no worse, they were no better, than other men, most of whom succumbed to temptation and opportunity.

Professor Rolleston seemed to entertain a similar apprehension. "With regard," he said, "to all absorbing studies, it is the besetting sin of them and of original research, that they lift a man so entirely above the ordinary sphere of daily duty that it betrays him (in other lines of original research as well as this) into selfishness and unscrupulous neglect of duty," and he added the testimony of an eminent professor. Mr. Skey, said he, wrote in his work, "A man who has the reputation of a splendid operator is ever a just object of suspicion." No doubt, for opportunity to such men was almost irresistible.

But these operations appeared to blunt the understanding in many as much as they hardened the heart. Some learned men had actually declared that animals were like puppets—they kicked, cried, and made a noise, but had no feeling whatever. Such was the attempted despotism of science over common sense. Others urged that animals were not to be pitied, because they had no foreknowledge of what was going to happen. But, if that was so, it was the best and most fearful argument he had ever heard, and one conducing to the issues just mentioned, for the vivisection of babies and idiots, for they would have no foreknowledge of the torture that awaited them. But the strongest part of the whole evidence to show the degradation of moral feeling was that of Dr. Klein, who was employed officially by the medical officer to the Privy Council. These were some of the questions put to him, and his answers to them :—

" When you say that you only use anæsthetics for convenience sake, do you mean that you have no regard at all to the sufferings of the animals ? " " No regard at all." " Then for your own purposes you disregard entirely the question of the suffering of the animal in performing a painful experiment ? " " I do." " But, in regard to your proceedings as an investigator, you are prepared to acknowledge that you hold as entirely indifferent the sufferings of the animal which is subjected to your investigation ? " " Yes." What could surpass or even equal such philosophy as that ?

And finally, a gentleman, whom he would not name, bore testimony to the " kindness " of Dr. Burdon-Sanderson and Dr. Klein. When interrogated " Whether he did not think that the habit of regarding animals as a mere battery of vital forces on which particular results are to be studied, necessarily to a certain extent produces the effect of diminishing the sympathy with their sufferings? " he said, " I think not. I do not know anywhere a kinder person than Dr. Burdon-Sanderson." " Or than Dr. Klein, for instance ? " asked the Commission. " I have no reason," said this gentleman, " to think otherwise of him." · That opinion, from such a person as the gentleman he would not name, completed his (Lord S.) conviction of the evil effects of those practices on a kind and generous nature. But to conclude, the subject was inexhaustible; it was impossible for him to compress within a small compass all the arguments that might be urged, and all the facts that might be adduced; but he was not pleading for total abolition, he was pleading only for mitigation of the system, and surely there was no wisdom in declaring that one evil shall continue to exist because another could not be put down. Up to this point scientific men were with the advocates of restriction. England had prohibited bull-baiting, cock-fighting, prize-fighting, all of which had, in their day, no end of logic and sentiment in their favour; and why should she not hold her place among all the nations of the earth, and be the first to reduce, within the closest possible limits, the sufferings inflicted by man on the whole animal creation?

THE second speech, the substance of which we reprint, was delivered in support of Lord Truro's Bill, in the House of Lords, 15th July, 1879:—

The Earl of SHAFTESBURY requested leave for a few words on this sad question. He said that, notwithstanding what had been urged in answer to the noble lord, that noble lord had done right in presenting a Bill for the total abolition of the practice of vivisection. Licences had been freely granted for painful experiments; for dispensing with anæsthetics, and with the obligation to kill the suffering animals after the experiment had been performed. Now, if this was done under the superintendence of a Secretary of State who had brought in the Bill, and who had ever declared himself, and truly, he believed, to be anxious for every possible abatement of the evil, what were they to expect from any one who might succeed him, and whose opinions, tinctured by the idolatry of the day, were that everything was to be sacrificed to the Image of science? No one, he believed, had laboured harder than himself to carry the present experimental Act. He had hoped much amelioration from it, but he found none; and more especially was he convinced of its inutility when he saw licences and certificates granted to Dr. Rutherford, whose abundant and cruel experiments were set out in the report of the Royal Commission, and who himself had declared that his experiments, to be conclusive, must be tried on the living man. That professor, moreover, did not stand very high in the medical world. His attention had been directed to the Hunterian oration by Dr. Moxon in 1877, in which the professor's doings were elaborately ridiculed, which remarks were endorsed and supported by many medical authorities. But the Act, he maintained, was not only useless, it was delusive and misleading. Many persons were lulled into a belief that by its provisions protection was afforded. So it was, no doubt; but it was protection to the vivisectors, and not to the animals. The noble Earl (Beauchamp) had enlarged on the security of anæsthetics. He (Lord S.) might ask on that point some preliminary questions. Were the anæsthetics administered at all? Were they carefully and accurately administered? What were they? Were they effective? Was it chloral? If so, a very weak application. Was it

curare? If so, and he said it on the authority of
the great vivisector, Claude Bernard, that it caused
more suffering than it attempted to prevent. Was
it morphia? Why that only utterly subdued the
victim, without deadening the pain. There was
much delusion in all these assurances; there was
little confidence to be placed in them.

But no fact had more influenced his judgment
than the announcement of a public memorial to the
well-known operator on animal life, M. Claude
Bernard. This memorial was supported by many
of the most scientific men in England, who testified
their admiration of his zeal and skill in this department of science. He asked permission to give one
specimen, out of many instances, perhaps hundreds,
of the deeds of that singular man. The extract
was taken from Claude Bernard's "Liquides de
l'Organisme," p. 40 :—

" We cut out the kidneys from a bull-dog [a pretty
statement to begin with]. Next day, twenty-four
hours after the operation, the dog, without being
enfeebled, appeared dejected, respiration was impeded,
and sighing. He had vomited during the night.
He refused all food and avoided movement, appeared
to suffer, and at times cried out. In order that his
cries should not disturb the neighbours we applied a
muzzle pretty tightly. [What a spirit of consideration
for the peace of the locality!] When during the
day we returned we found the dog lying dead, his
muzzle bathed in a fetid fluid, which he had vomited.
The muzzle had hindered the expulsion of the
vomiting and caused the animal to be suffocated by
it." Such was the man that the philosophers
delighted to honour!

And that was the work of science!—of that which
its worshippers called science—and among the

promoters of the memorial might be found some who had testified, in the strongest manner, against the infliction of needless pain, and the practice of mere speculative vivisection. What then could be a fuller proof of a cruel and morbid curiosity, and what hope remained that investigators and operators, delighting in such things, would respect the principle, and be restrained within the limitations of the Act?

Now further he observed that since the passing of the Act, as well as before, many learned lectures had been delivered and many learned treatises published denying altogether the value of vivisection; nay more, maintaining that the results were fallacious and more likely to lead to error than to truth. The contradictions of vivisectionists were surprising. They agreed in nothing but that the animals should be cut up. Now, the three following questions had been propounded and admirably handled in a recent work by Dr. Gimson:—

"1. Have vivisections and painful experiments been of any scientific value? 2. Have they led to the discovery of scientific facts of permanent importance? 3. Are there not fallacies underlying such a method of interrogating Nature, which of necessity vitiate the results?"

Many sound and really scientific men were prepared to say "No" to the first two questions, and "Yes" to the third; and most justly too. For was it not manifest that safe and accurate conclusions could not be drawn from examinations of an animal reduced to such an abnormal state? Were it placed under an anæsthetic, would not all its internal functions—he did not pretend to use professional language—be altered or suspended thereby, so as utterly to nullify all close and reliable deductions as to what might be the case in its natural and ordinary state? Was it under the operation of the knife, pure and simple—would not the pain, the terror of the wretched victim, render the conclusions still more fallacious? The vivisectors, many of them, felt the force of the argument. To evade it, they asserted (and nevertheless had the audacity to call themselves masters in science) that the poor animal whined and winced, and gave every indication of suffering, but that it was hard, dull, insensible. Others, claiming some portion of humanity, rejoiced that the animals had no forethought at least of the tortures that awaited them; an argument, which if of any value at all, might, in their zealous regard for the comfort of the human race, be brought to bear on the vivisection of idiots and babies.

But scientific men of this stamp should be listened to when deploring their own ill success. What said the famous Claude Bernard? Why, after thirty years of operations on living animals he confessed: "Our hands, without doubt, are empty to-day, but our mouths full, it may be, of legitimate promises for the future;" and he said no more, but yet that was the sole result of countless experiments of the most cruel description. And what said Mr. Rutherford? He, Lord Shaftesbury, must again refer to him. "His experiments," he allowed, "were only suggestive of inferences, which, to become conclusive, would require the experiments to be tried on man." Exactly so; but what then has been gained by this almost unprecedented torture of animals? Why, the important admission that continued experiments are useless, and that man himself must be subjected to torture before that professor could arrive at a conclusion. And yet to this professor had the power been renewed of the free and fruitless use of the knife! The vivisection of man was no new thought;

the proposition had once been made by the great professor Cheselden, and was rejected solely because public opinion was not then ripe for such a step in scientific pursuit.

He was happy to state that resistance was spreading rapidly, and extending through all parts of Europe and in America. Associations had been formed in France, in Italy, in Germany, and in Russia, for the total suppression of vivisection. Persons of all ranks and degrees, professors and learned men, were at the head of those associations, and much good had already been effected at Alfort and at Florence by their combined exertions.

It was impossible, he said, in discussing this question, to avoid the repetition of old arguments and the production of similar instances. The opponents of the system urged, and urged truly, the brutalizing effects on the minds of the vivisectors, and on the minds of those who approved them. He would quote, in brief, but one instance, but it was a striking one, and he implored their lordships to listen to it—it was extracted from an address delivered at Dresden by Baron Ernest von Weber, who took it from the work of Professor Goltz, of the Physiological Institution at Strasburg:—"A very clever, lively young female dog, which had learnt to shake hands with both fore-paws had the left side of the brain washed out through two holes on the 1st of December, 1875. [He begged them to mark the coolness and evident pleasure with which he thus treated his pet companion.] This caused lameness in the right paw. On being asked for the left, the dog immediately lays it in my hand. I now demand the right, but the creature only looks at me sorrowfully, for it cannot move it. [Did their lordships observe how he relished his barbarous experiments?] On my continuing to press for it, the dog crosses the left paw over and offers it to me on the right side, as if to make amends for not being able to give the right. [Without that fact, recorded on such authority, would it have been thought possible that an educated man should have been insensible to such an appeal? But he was so, and, revelling in his science, he prolonged his amusement.] On the 13th of January a second portion of the brain was destroyed. [But that was not enough.] On the 15th of February a third, and on the 6th of March a fourth, this last operation causing death." Thus, to gratify the peculiar taste of the inhuman wretch, that poor little animal was kept under torture and examination, as foolish as it was ferocious, from the 1st of December to the 6th of March, a period of more than three months!

Now, in what way, he asked, was true science advanced by such curious and refined cruelty? In what way was man benefited or knowledge blessed by such discoveries? And yet these were the certain and necessary consequences of legalised vivisection. Scientific men, he said, and, indeed, others, who ought to know better, were pleased to talk of the "lower animals." In what sense was the epithet "lower" to be applied to that affectionate little thing? Had their lordships observed its unabated attachment to its cold-blooded master? Had they not been struck by its spirit of forgiveness under treatment so cruel? Had they not seen an exhibition of qualities that would have become a thinking being? And that was the use they made of the creatures committed to their charge! that the account they would render of their stewardship! All he could say was—and he said it truly and conscientiously—that in every respect he would infinitely rather be the dog than be the professor. (Hear, hear.) But whether the law was efficient or inefficient, whether vivisection was conducive to science or the reverse, there was one great preliminary consideration : On what authority of Scripture, or any other form of revelation, he asked most solemnly, did they rest their right to subject God's creatures to such unspeakable sufferings ? The thought had troubled the mind of many vivisectors ; it had deeply touched the heart of Sir Charles Bell. That they might take the life of animals for food, or to remove danger or annoyance, he fully admitted ; but he utterly denied that they were permitted to indulge their curiosity or even advance their knowledge by the infliction of exquisite torture on the sentient creation. They were told in haughty and dogmatic style that the secrets of nature could be learnt in no other way. Learned in no other way ! Could it be believed that the Almighty had issued such a decree ? The animals were His creatures as much as we were His creatures ; and " His tender mercies." so the Bible told us, " were over all His works." He, along with many, repudiated such an atrocious and shallow doctrine ; and under that conviction he would ever do his best to put down a system that was as needless as it was cruel.

www.ingramcontent.com/pod-product-compliance
Lightning Source LLC
Chambersburg PA
CBHW021246260626
47172CB00002B/863